Pig & Toad

Best Friends Forever

written by Dayle Quigley

illustrated by Sara Weingartner

BEAVER'S
POND
PRESS

ISBN: 978-1-59298-486-2

Library of Congress Catalog Number: 2012910051

Printed in the United States of America

First Printing: 2012

15 14 13 12   4 3 2 1

Edited by Kellie Hultgren and Lily Coyle
Illustrations, cover and interior design by Sara Weingartner

BEAVER'S
POND
PRESS

Beaver's Pond Press, Inc.
7108 Ohms Lane
Edina, MN 55439-2129
(952) 829-8818
www.BeaversPondPress.com

To order, visit www.BeaversPondBooks.com or call 1-800-901-3480. Reseller discounts available.

www.pigandtoad.com

Dear Ms. Quigley,

Polka dots are important
because without them
white dresses would be lonely.

Michael
6th grade

For my friends,
you are the polka dots
on my white dress.
–DQ

For Claire and Benjamin,
who have been best friends
since the moment they met.
–SJW

Chapter 1

Toad's Big Concert

"Today is the day," thought Pig. "I am so happy! Today Toad comes to town."

Pig and Toad had been friends for a very, very long time, but Toad had been away. Pig missed her friend. But today—yes, today!—that was changing. Toad was coming to give a concert. He was a singer when he wasn't just being a toad.

"Everyone will be there to see Toad," Pig thought, "but Toad will find me because we're best buddies. He'll wink and smile at me, and when he sings I'll know he is singing for me!"

And so Pig smiled as she got ready for the concert. She washed her face until it shone. She put on her favorite sparkly tutu. And she practiced her exuberant wave and cheer so that Toad could find her in the crowd.

Pig took her seat in the middle of the auditorium. She sat up very straight and tall so that Toad could see her. But when he walked onto the stage, he did not wink. "Oh," thought Pig, "maybe he can't see me."

Fortunately, Pig had planned for this. She reached beneath her seat and pulled out her sign. Surely Toad would see it and smile a big Toad smile.

But he did not. "Oh," thought Pig, "Hmm. Maybe he cannot see my sign."

Fortunately, Pig had planned for this, also.
When the song ended and the audience
applauded, Pig waved and cheered exuberantly.
"Hip-hip-hooray, Toad! Way to go, Toad! Here I
am. It is me, Pig." But Toad did not wink at Pig or
smile at her or sing her a special song.

"Oh," thought Pig, "maybe he did not hear me." Pig was maybe just a wee bit less happy.

"It doesn't matter. I will see Toad after the concert," she told herself.

After the show, Pig went out to the stage door and waited. Toad did not come out. "Hmm," thought Pig, "I wonder what is holding up Toad." Pig checked the stage and the bathroom. Then she looked outside for Toad's bicycle. "Hmm," thought Pig, "Toad doesn't go anywhere without his bicycle. He must have left. He left without seeing me, his best friend. Maybe he has forgotten me!"

The town was having a party for their famous singer, but Pig did not go. Pig walked home alone. Her face did not shine, and her tutu drooped.

"Tomorrow I will be happy," she thought, "but today I am a sad Pig."

At home, she sat in her favorite chair and ate her favorite cookies. But the chair was uncomfortable and the cookies seemed stale. She went outside to smell the flowers and look at the stars, but the flowers had no scent and the stars did not twinkle.

Meanwhile, Toad was wondering what had happened to Pig. By the time he came out from backstage, Pig was nowhere to be found. "Perhaps she will be at the party," Toad thought. But no, she was not there. "Maybe she is very sick," he thought. "That would be horrible!"

Toad got on his bicycle and raced to Pig's house. There he found Pig looking very sad.

"Pig, are you sick?" asked Toad.

"No," said Pig, "I am sad."

"If you are not sick," asked Toad, "why didn't you come to my party?"

"I thought you had forgotten me," she said.

Toad looked puzzled. "Why would you think that?"

"I sat up very straight and tall at the concert so you would see me, but you didn't wink at me," said Pig.

"I did look for you," said Toad, "but all I saw were cows."

"And when you sang, I held up my special sign very high, but you did not smile at me," said Pig.

"Pig," said Toad, "the stage lights were so bright I couldn't see your sign."

"Oh," said Pig, feeling a wee bit foolish. "But after the concert, I waited for you. I looked for you outside and on the stage and in the bathroom. I couldn't find you or your bicycle. You never go anywhere without your bicycle."

"Pig," said Toad, "I was in the dressing room, taking off my makeup. It takes a lot of makeup for people to see me onstage. My bicycle was with me."

"Oh," said Pig, now feeling very foolish. "So are you still my friend, Toad?"

"Of course," said Toad. "We will always be friends!"

"Good," exclaimed Pig, jumping up and grabbing Toad's hand. "Let's go to the party!" And off they went.

Chapter 2

The Carnival

"The carnival is coming! The carnival is coming!" sang Pig all the way to Toad's house. She loved the carnival: the face-painting, the cotton candy, the rides. It was all wonderful.

"Toad! Toad!" yelled Pig when she arrived at Toad's house. "The carnival is coming! Isn't that great? Isn't that wonderful?" Pig danced around as she asked, "Will you go with me, Toad?"

"I can't go. I am practicing my singing," said Toad.

"You can practice tomorrow," said Pig.

"I was planning on riding my bicycle today," said Toad.

"You can ride your bicycle to the carnival," said Pig.

"I don't like the carnival," replied Toad. "It scares me."

"Oh," said Pig. "Will you go with me anyway? There are lots of beautiful things at the carnival, and I will protect you."

"Okay," said Toad reluctantly.

Toad went into his house and put on his jacket. He found his favorite helmet and placed it neatly on his head. Then he turned out the lights and shut the front door. All the while he kept saying to himself, "I will have fun."

Toad rode his bicycle and Pig skipped and sang all the way to the carnival.

The carnival was everything Pig knew it would be. There were bands playing. There were games to try. There were rides to ride and treats to eat.

"Isn't this wonderful, Toad?" said Pig. "Let's go ride the Ferris wheel."

"I don't ride Ferris wheels," said Toad.

"Why not?" asked Pig.

"That's only for little toads," he answered.

"Maybe later," said Pig.

"Maybe," said Toad.

"Let's get our faces painted," said Pig.

"I don't get my face painted," said Toad.

"Oh," said Pig. "Well, I do." And with that, Pig marched over to the face-painter. She did not get just a little flower or star. She picked a design for her entire face.

"Isn't it beautiful?" said Pig. She thought she saw just the slightest smile on Toad's face.

"Do you want to ride the Ferris wheel now?" asked Pig. "I bet the carnival is beautiful from up high."

"No," said Toad. "I do not want to ride the Ferris wheel. But I will go on the bumper cars."

"Yippee!" said Pig.

Pig drove fast. She went clockwise and

counterclockwise. She rammed into every car.

Toad put on his seat belt. He only went in one direction. He stayed away from the other cars, and when he hit someone, he said he was sorry.

When the ride was over, Pig was jumping up and down with excitement, and Toad was smiling his nice Toad smile.

"How about now, Toad? Will you go on the Ferris wheel now?" asked Pig.

"I don't like Ferris wheels," said Toad.

"Have you ever been on a Ferris wheel?" asked Pig.

Toad looked at his feet. "No," he mumbled.

"Oh, Toad," said Pig, "You have to go on the Ferris wheel! You'll love it. I promise."

"Okay," said Toad, "but can we get ice cream first?"

"Of course," said Pig.

Toad got vanilla, and Pig got vanilla chocolate twist with sprinkles. Then they got into line for the Ferris wheel.

"Toad, this is going to be so much fun!" said Pig. "We will go up high and see all the lights down below. We will go around and around. I am so excited!"

Toad did not look very excited. In fact, Toad looked a little greener than normal.

Finally it was their turn. Pig could hardly get in fast enough. Toad took his time. Pig squealed with delight. Toad held on tight and wished for the ride to be over. He wanted to look, but he just couldn't.

The Ferris wheel went around and around. Pig and Toad went up and down. Toad kept his eyes shut tight.

Then the Ferris wheel stopped with Pig and Toad at the very top.

"Oh, Toad," said Pig, "open your eyes!"

"I can't," said Toad, "I am too scared."

"Sure you can," said Pig. "I'll help. That's what friends are for."

Slowly Pig peeled Toad's fingers away from his eyes. Toad said nothing for a long time. Then he whispered, "It's marvelous!" and a smile spread across his face.

The Ferris wheel started moving again. It went around and around. Pig and Toad went up and down, and this time Toad saw it all. When the ride was over, he turned to Pig and said, "Can we do it again?"

"Yes!" said Pig, "As many times as you want."

As they rode, Toad began to hum, then sing.

"What are you singing?" asked Pig

"My new song, 'Fear of Heights,'" said Toad.

"Oh," said Pig, "I think we should change the title."

"Maybe," said Toad, and he kept on singing.

Chapter 3

Pig's Birthday

One morning Toad opened his eyes and climbed out of bed as he always did. He washed his face and brushed his teeth as he did every day. He ate his breakfast and made his bed as though it were a regular day. But today was not like every other day. Today was Pig's birthday.

Toad had been getting ready for weeks now. He had spent long hours deciding what to get Pig. He thought about getting her chocolate. Pig loved chocolate. He thought about getting her a bicycle. He knew *he* would like that as a gift.

After thinking for a long time, he decided to get Pig a beautiful blue tutu with yellow polka dots and a matching scarf. He carefully wrapped his gift and tied a beautiful bow around it. Pig was having a big party that evening. Toad would give her the present then.

Toad called her up and said, "Good morning, Pig. Happy birthday!"

"Thank you, Toad!" said Pig.

"Are you ready for the party? Can I help?" asked Toad.

"I am all ready," said Pig. "The cake is baked. The table is set. And I am wearing my new blue tutu with yellow polka dots. It is marvelous. I liked it so much that I got you a scarf to match!"

Toad swallowed hard. "Oh," he said. "That's great. I'll see you tonight."

Toad slumped into his chair. What was he going to do now? His wonderful present was no longer wonderful.

Then it came to him. He would get her a bouquet of flowers. Pig loved flowers. Off he went to pick sunflowers, her favorite. But when Toad got to Pig's house, his happy smile faded away. Vases and buckets and watering cans filled with sunflowers surrounded Pig's house.

Pig came dancing out the front door.

"Hello, Toad," said Pig. "What are you doing here? The party is not until tonight."

"Uh, umm," said Toad, hiding the flowers behind his back. "I was coming to see if you needed help."

"No, I am all ready," said Pig.

"See you tonight, then," said Toad, slowly backing away.

Toad trudged home. What was he going to do now? He had no present and no more ideas.

He sat in his chair and thought of Pig in her tutu. He saw her birthday crown perched on her head. He saw the flowers and the big chocolate cake. "But," he thought, "I didn't see balloons." A smile crept across his face.

Away he went on his bicycle. He got balloons of every color in the rainbow. He was so excited that he pedaled right over to Pig's house.

"Pig! Pig!" called Toad. "Come outside!"

Pig came bounding out the door. "Oh!" she exclaimed. "For me? Oh, Toad, thank you!"

Pig reached out to take the balloons from Toad. Toad began singing "Happy Birthday" in his very best singing voice and stretched out his arm to give the balloons to Pig. But he opened his hand too soon.

Toad and Pig stared into the sky as the balloons flew away. Toad stopped singing and let out a very long, sad sigh.

"Pig," he said, "I am so sorry. I can't do anything right." But Pig wore a gigantic smile on her face. He followed her gaze back up into the sky.

"Toad," she said, "you put
a hundred polka dots in the sky.
This is the best birthday present ever!"
    At that, Toad began to sing again.

Pig Grows Up

Pig bounced with excitement as she hung up her posters. She had big posters and little posters. She hung them on trees and bulletin boards and lampposts and fences. She was hanging up the very last poster when she ran into Toad.

"What are you doing?" asked Toad.

"I'm having a concert," said Pig, very proud of herself. "I've decided to be a singer like you."

"But you are already a singer," said Toad.
"You sing a lot."

"I want to be a grown-up singer," answered
Pig. "I need to sing on a stage."

Toad thought Pig was being a little silly. But
all he said was, "That's wonderful, Pig!"

"Can you come, Toad?" asked Pig with a
wishful look on her face.

"I would like to," said Toad, "but I will be
away. I can help you get ready, though. I can
teach you everything I know about grown-up
singing."

"Oh, thank you, Toad!" said Pig. "Let's start
right now."

Toad taught Pig how to warm up her voice with "la la la la." He taught her how to take a deep breath in and then let it out before starting. They practiced standing up straight and tall. And, most importantly, they practiced standing still. Pig liked to skip and twirl when she sang, but that is not the grown-up way to sing.

When the big day came, Pig put on her special concert tutu. She liked how it glimmered when she twirled. She skipped all the way to the hall, warming up her voice with "la la la la." She thought about breathing and standing up straight and tall. She reminded herself about standing still. Most of all, she thought about how much fun it was going to be.

"I am going to be a grown-up singer just like Toad," thought Pig.

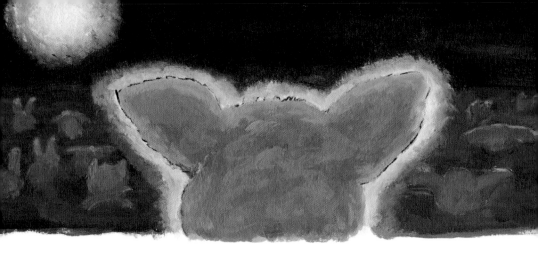

Finally, the moment came and Pig walked out onto the stage.

"Oh," she thought, "there are a lot of people in the audience." She took a deep breath in and then let it out.

"Oh," she thought, "it is very hot up here on the stage."

She opened her mouth to sing, but nothing came out. She tried again, and again there was nothing. The audience was very quiet.

"Uh-oh, Toad did not tell me what to do if I

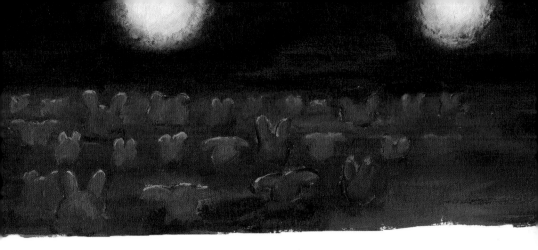

lost my voice. I did not practice this," thought Pig. "I do not like this grown-up singing!"

Suddenly Pig heard Toad's voice inside her head. "Sing out, Pig. You can do this! You sing beautifully."

Pig tried one more time, and this time music came out! Pig sang all of her favorite songs: "Impossible" and "You Can Fly" and "Rainbow Connection," and best of all, "Dazzling Blue." At the end, Pig took a big bow and ran offstage. She was very happy to be behind the curtains again.

When Toad got home from his trip, he came to see Pig.

"How did it go, Pig? Did you like grown-up singing? Tell me all about it," said Toad. Pig told him about how it was hot onstage and how she lost her voice. Then she told him about finding her voice and singing her favorite songs.

"But I don't think I will be a grown-up singer," said Pig.

"You don't like being a grown-up singer?" asked Toad.

"No," said Pig, "It isn't for me. My songs are not the same when I don't skip and twirl."

"I suppose not," said Toad with a twinkle in his eyes. "I do believe some singers aren't meant to stand still."

Chapter 5

Snow Day

Toad's phone rang. "Good morning," he answered.

"Good morning," said Pig. "Would you like to come over for a snow day?"

"There is no snow outside," said Toad, looking out the window. "It is a beautiful, warm day."

"I know," said Pig. "But I love snow days. So I'm going to pretend there's snow outside. I can see it building up already."

"I'm on my way!" Toad grabbed earmuffs and hopped on his bicycle. "Pig has the best ideas," he thought.

When Toad arrived, Pig was sitting on the porch with her scarf wrapped around her neck. She looked very cold.

"Toad," she said, "I'm so glad you made it before the storm got bad. It's much more fun to share a snow day. Let's go make snow angels."

"Oh, it has been a long time since I made snow angels," said Toad. "They will be beautiful in this new snow."

Pig and Toad lay down in the grass. They moved their arms up and down to make angel wings and moved their legs back and forth to make angel gowns. They made two angels, and then they made two more and then two more. Pig's smile grew with each new set of angels. Finally the lawn was covered with winged shapes.

"That was great," said Toad. "What should we do now?"

"We're going skiing," answered Pig, "so jump on the ski lift."

Pig and Toad climbed the steps to Pig's porch and jumped on the swing. The swing swayed as the friends traveled up the mountainside.

"We're at the top," said Toad. "Let's jump off together on three. One, two, three!" Pig and Toad jumped off the ski lift and into the grass.

"Okay," said Pig. "You go first." Pig ran over and started a fan blowing. She wanted Toad to feel the wind as he raced down the hill.

Away Toad went! He was an amazing skier.
He skied on just his right leg and then his left. He
went over a jump and did a flip in the air. He even
went down part of the hill backwards. When he
made it to the bottom, he yelled to Pig, "Your turn."

Pig steadied herself on her skis and started down the hill. She skied on just her right leg and then her left. She did a flip in the air and began to ski down the hill backwards. But then she tumbled over and over again.

Toad began to laugh. "Oh Pig," he said. "You look like a giant snowball."

"Thanks," she said, jumping up. "Now, Toad, it's time for the blizzard. I will go into the cornfield and pretend it's a blizzard. I will yell 'Toad, Toad, where are you?' and you will yell 'Pig, Pig I am here,' and I will find my way out. Okay?"

Toad wasn't sure that was a good idea. He said, "Okay, Pig. But don't wait too long to start calling. You don't want to get lost."

Off Pig went into the cornfield, skipping and singing. She went in circles and wavy lines. She wanted to get a little lost so that the blizzard would seem real.

Toad sat on the porch and listened to Pig's singing. Finally, when he could barely hear her, he began to call out.

"Pig, Pig, where are you?" Pig did not answer. Toad called out louder, "Pig, Pig, I am over here. Can you hear me?"

Pig did not answer, and Toad began to worry. He paced as he called out to Pig. He called out even louder. He was working so hard at pacing and calling, he didn't notice Pig until she burst out of the cornfield with a grin on her face.

"Oh, Pig," said Toad, "I'm glad you're safe. I was worried. Were you scared, lost and alone in the cornfield?"

Pig looked surprised. "I wasn't alone."

"You weren't alone?" Toad asked.

"No," she said. "You were with me. I always take you with me, Toad. Right here." And she pointed to her heart. "Thanks for going along."

Toad shook his head and smiled. He didn't tell Pig, but he never went anywhere without her, either. Instead, he said, "Pig, let's go inside and have hot chocolate."

Pig's eyes grew wide. "Hot chocolate with marshmallows! Lots of marshmallows and whipped cream and chocolate sauce," she said. "I love hot chocolate!"

"And I do, too." said Toad.

About the Author

Dayle Quigley lives in Hayward, Wisconsin. When not skipping and singing, she is an ER physician, and director of NorthWoods Strings. Her children are still waiting for her to grow up.

About the Illustrator

Sara Weingartner lives in Minneapolis, Minnesota with her husband and two children. She has loved drawing since she was a little girl. "It has been pure joy bringing *Pig and Toad* to life." Visit more of Sara's work at CreativeSoulDesign.com.